PLEASANT BOOKS IN EASY ENGLISH

STAGE 1

Dead or Alive?
and other stories

PLEASANT BOOKS IN EASY ENGLISH

STAGE 1

Dead or Alive?
and other stories

by

G. C. Thornley

LONGMAN

LONGMAN GROUP LIMITED
London

*Associated companies, branches and representatives
throughout the world*

© Longman Group Ltd 1969

*First published *1969*
*New impressions *December 1970; *September 1971*

ISBN 0 582 53157 8

Illustrated by Glenys Sida

*Printed in Hong Kong by
The Hong Kong Printing Press Ltd*

Contents

WAR NEWS   1
FATHERS AND SONS   17
IN THE TRAIN   21
HOW DID HE DO IT?   31
DEAD OR ALIVE?   42

Foreword

THE books of this series are intended for those who have left the age of fairy-tales behind them, but require some reading material in easy English.

The vocabulary of Stage 1 is limited to about 480 of the commonest words in English. The tenses used in the Active Voice exclude the Past Perfect and the Future Perfect, the more complicated continuous tenses, and all the more difficult constructions expressing uncertainty. In the Passive Voice the tenses are, for the most part, limited to the Present and the Past.

The subordinate clauses introduced into the text include only simple relative and adverbial clauses. Noun clauses, if used at all, are very rare.

War News

In a room in Colport there was a big table made of beautiful wood. Two men were sitting at the table and talking quietly.

'We'll have to send Cunningham,' Miller said. He was the smaller of the two men. Miller was not his true name, but everyone called him that.

'Why Cunningham?' Goddard asked. 'Why not someone else?' Goddard was a fat man, and he took his coat off as he spoke. It was a hot day.

'Because he's not too fat,' Miller said, looking at Goddard's fat arms. 'And there isn't anyone else.'

'I don't like that man,' Goddard said. 'He asks too many questions, and he can't think. Why don't you go yourself?'

'Oh, I don't like that kind of thing,' Miller answered. 'No. Cunningham's the only man who can do this. We must send him. Why not? Why do we pay him? He never does much for us. We must make him work for his money.'

The two men were talking about some papers which they wanted to get. The papers had some notes on them – notes about ships. They were in another house in Colport. A lot of men worked in that house, and there was a girl too. Other people could never get in. When they tried, someone always stopped them.

'You may be right,' Goddard said. 'I'm too fat to go myself. I can't get over walls or run quickly if anyone sees me.'

'You can't,' said Miller. 'You're not the right man to do it.'

'So will you talk to Cunningham? Tell him about the papers and the wall and everything else. He doesn't know anything about that house, does he? Does he even know the way to it?'

'No, he doesn't. So I'll tell him everything.' Miller stood up and left the room and the house. He walked along the road to his own house, went in, and telephoned to Cunningham.

'Come to see me here at once,' Miller said.

Soon after this a car stopped outside Miller's house, and a man with a red face and blue eyes came into the room. Miller looked at him coldly.

'Sit down,' said Miller. 'You and I were talking about some papers yesterday – papers with some notes on them. Remember?'

'About ships?' Cunningham asked.

'That's right. About ships. Their names and everything about them. We want those papers tonight. You will get them for us. They have the names of the ships on them.' He stood up and looked through the window; but there was no one outside, and he sat down again.

'Where are the papers?' Cunningham asked. 'Can't you get them yourself?'

'No. You're the man who's going to get them; and you're going to get them tonight.'

'Where are they?' Cunningham asked again.

'In that house with the big windows on the hill. It's called *Mandalay*. You've seen it sometimes.'

'I've never seen it,' said Cunningham. 'Which side of the hill? There are lots of houses on the hill. How can I find it?'

'It's in Ash Street. You can see its wall from the trains when you go to London.'

'What wall?'

'You're asking too many questions. I'm tired of them.'

Cunningham stood up. 'If you don't want to tell me about the wall, I'll go home.' He walked to the door.

'Come back!' cried Miller angrily. 'Sit down there!'

Cunningham sat down again and looked at Miller's face. He did not like Miller's face.

'There's a big wall at the side of the road,' Miller said. 'You'll see it when you go up the hill. Walk up Ash Street and look for a high wall, and that's *Mandalay*.'

'How can I get over the wall?'

'You must find a way yourself. You're young and strong.'

'If I get over it, what shall I do? Where are the papers that you want? Who has them? Which room? You tell me nothing.'

'They'll be in Carlton's room near the front door,' said Miller. He spoke quietly. He had to make Cunningham do this, and so he must not make the man angry. 'I call it Carlton's room, but that girl does a lot of work there too.'

'What's her name?'

'Mary Relf. She's the only girl that works there. All the others in the house are men. And there are always two other men outside, near the high wall, ready to catch thieves. Remember them, my dear Cunningham, and take care. They're men who shoot first and ask their questions later. Don't let them see you. If they see you in there, you're a dead man. The country's at war. Remember that.'

'What do they all do in that place?' Cunningham asked.

'Oh, they talk about ships – the ships that bring food here and take guns to Africa. We want to send them all to the bottom of the sea. I don't have to tell you that. So we have to find them, don't we? The men who work in that house don't talk much. We mustn't ask them anything. If we do that, the police will come to see us. But we can find the ships on the sea if we can get some news of them; and then we can send them to the bottom.'

'What do you want to know about the ships?'

'Everything, my dear man. How many ships will go? Big or small? What are their names? When will they leave Britain? At what time? From where? London? Liverpool? Bristol? Glasgow? What are they carrying? Where will they take it? All that kind of thing.'

'And how can I get this news for you?'

'It isn't very hard. The best way is to get the notes which Mary Relf writes. The men in that house meet and talk about the ships. The girl, Mary Relf, goes to the meetings and takes notes. They must have notes because there are a lot of things to remember. They have to remember times, names of ships, kinds of guns and things like that. And they have to send some news to the newspapers too, but they never send any news that can help anyone. Mary Relf herself takes care of the newspapers. She writes her notes at the meeting and then takes them to Carlton's room, in the front of the house. She works there alone, after the others have gone home. She changes the notes there and writes something for the newspapers.'

'Why must she tell the newspapers anything at all?' Cunningham asked.

'Oh, you know the newspapers. They always want news. If they get none, they make trouble. So Mary Relf gets something ready for them, but it doesn't say much. She leaves out the names of ships and places, and other things, too. So they get no names, no days, no times. So we don't want those notes. We want the full notes which she writes at the meeting. The full notes, remember! Get them before she goes home. You'll never find them if you're late.'

'When does she go home?' Cunningham asked.

'When she has finished. I don't know the time.'

'How can I get the papers? I can't just walk into the house and take them from her table. Can't you stand under a window when they're having a meeting? You can hear something then.'

'If I stand there,' Miller said, 'I'll hear nothing. I've tried it before. They always talk very quietly. and they all sit in a big room, far away from the window and the door and the walls. And the meeting's finished now. They had their meeting this afternoon.'

'Why can't your men find the ships on the sea, after they leave Britain?'

'You're asking too many questions,' said Miller angrily, looking into Cunningham's blue eyes. 'You know nothing at all about the sea, do you? It's a big place, my friend. We have to know something about the ships' journeys. A ship may be on its way to Canada. If our men look for it near Africa, what will they see? Water, and nothing else. So get those papers tonight, and then we can send the ships to the bottom.'

'Why tonight? Can't I try tomorrow?'

'They had a long meeting this afternoon. So Mary Relf will be in that room tonight. She'll take her notes there. You must get them. Sometimes she burns them when she has finished.'

'How shall I know the right papers?' Cunningham asked.

'I can't tell you. You'll have to think about that yourself. But the words at the top of the papers may

5

help. One of the words will be SHIPS or something like that.'

Cunningham did not look pleased. This was going to be hard.

'She'll stop me if I try to take the papers,' he said.

'Yes, she will. You'll have to get her out of the room in some way or other – or kill her. Remember the war.'

'I'm not going to kill her or anyone else,' said Cunningham angrily. 'I'm not going to touch her – not for any money.'

'If she sees you, she'll cry out. But if she's dead, she can't. If she cries out, one of those men outside will hear her and run in. Then you'll be dead yourself in no time. He may even shoot you from outside. He'll see you through the window.'

'How nice!' Cunningham cried. 'Thanks! Why do I work for you? Why don't I stay at home like you?'

'Because you want our money. We pay you well, don't we? But you'll have to take care. They're always watching, always ready. If you make a noise, the men will find you at once, and shoot. So keep quiet. Don't make a sound. Wait for a train.'

'A train? Why?'

'Trains make noises. Get over the wall when a train's coming. The line there isn't far from the wall. Then the men may not hear you, and you may live to see to-morrow's sun.'

'Many, many thanks,' said Cunningham, standing up. 'If I see tomorrow's sun, I'll thank you again.'

He left Miller's house angrily, got into his car, and went to the station. He soon found Ash Street and walked quietly up the hill, looking at the names of the houses. At last he found *Mandalay*, and stopped under some trees to think.

The bottom part of the house was hidden from the

road by a high wall. How could he get over it?

In one place there was a tree not far from the wall. He went to look at it. He could get up the tree with a lot of trouble. But he could not jump from the top of the tree to the top of the wall. It was too far.

He went back home, had some dinner, changed his clothes and found his gun. He never wanted to shoot people; but this was war, and he had to be ready for anything. He went out of the back door and looked at some pieces of wood on the ground outside. One was a strong piece, and it was long too. It was part of an old tree.

'I can stand or sit on that,' he thought. 'I'll take it.'

He waited for some time, and then carried the piece of wood to the car. He put it on the top, got into the car himself, and went back to the bottom end of Ash Street. There he got out and carried the piece of wood to the tree.

There was not much light there, and no one saw him. After a lot of trouble, he was able to pull the wood to the top of the tree. The tree was hard, but he waited up there for some time. He heard a man walking quietly at the other side of the wall, but he did not see him.

From the top of the tree he could see the house. The men left the house and went home; their day's work was done. But Mary Relf did not come out of the house. She still had some work to do.

Cunningham heard the sound of a train coming along the line. He looked down at the street, but there was no one in it. When the train was near, he put one end of the piece of wood on the top of the wall. He kept the other end on the tree.

The train stopped at the station. Cunningham sat down on the wood, putting one foot at each side of it.

7

He waited up there for some time

Then he pulled himself quietly from the tree to the wall. He made some noise, but not much. He sat there on the wall and waited, but no one heard anything because the train was making noises not far away.

He looked down the side of the wall, but he could not see the two men. It was a long way down to the ground, and he did not want to jump, but what else could he do?

He looked along the wall to the left and saw something down on the ground there. So he moved quietly along the top of the wall, keeping his head down. When he was nearer, he could see some cars down there, and one of them was not far from the wall. He was able to put one foot on the top of the car, and he soon got down to the ground. But it gave him a lot of trouble.

He hid under a tree and waited, but he heard no cries or other sounds. Nothing happened, and he did not see the two men. So he moved quietly away to the front of the house, hiding under trees when he could. He stopped near a window. It was the window of Carlton's room, where the girl worked. He had to be quick. He must get those notes before she finished her day's work. He could see her at work.

He left the window and had a look at the other windows of the house. He moved very quietly all the time. Near the back he found one window which was partly open. He turned his head, saw no one and quietly got into the house. Then he shut the window. He did not want one of those men to see an open window.

He was in a room with white walls and with one or two wooden tables and chairs in it. He left it and found his way quietly to the door of Carlton's room at the front of the house. The door was shut, but he could hear someone in the room. The door of the

He could see her at work

next room was open, and he looked inside. It was a small room for coats.

He left the two doors and went to the back of the house again. He stood in the room with white walls, and kept the door open. Then he hit the top of the biggest table once with a chair. He did this as noisily as he could, and then called out, 'Mary Relf! Oooooh! Mary! Mary! Come quickly! Oooooh!'

The sounds were as sad as he could make them. After that, he ran quietly to the front of the house and hid himself in the room with coats in it.

He waited.

Mary Relf opened the door of her room and looked out.

'Anyone there?' she called, and waited for an answer.

There was no answer. So she came out of her room and went off to the back of the house.

Cunningham at once went into her room and looked at all the papers on her table. There were a lot. He had not much time, and he moved them about angrily with his hands. Then he heard the girl coming back, and at the same time he saw some words in big letters at the top of one of the papers:

WAR MEETING SQP 507 (SHIPS)

'There it is!' he thought gladly. Mary Relf was very near. He took the paper from the table and ran back quietly to the coats. She went into her room again and shut the door.

He ran as quietly as he could to the back of the house. He got out quickly through the same window and ran to the high wall. He got on the top of a car, and after some trouble got on the top of the wall again.

Mary Relf sat down to start work, but she could not find one of her papers. She looked again, but it was not on the table or on the floor. She could not believe her eyes at first, because it was there before.

Then she began to think about the noise in the house, and she was a quick thinker. Something was happening, and she could not understand it. She did not like things that she could not understand.

She opened the window and looked out into the night. She could not see the two men, and so she called out.

'Thieves! Thieves!' she cried. 'They've stolen a paper. Thieves! Catch them!'

One of the men heard her and ran to the window. She told him about the lost paper and the noise in the house. He ran off to look for the thief, calling to the other man at the same time.

Cunningham was now moving quietly along the top of the wall to the piece of wood near the tree. He wanted to get down and go far away from this place.

11

He heard angry cries from one end of the house, and then the sound of feet on the ground. A man called out, 'Catch him! Can you see anything? Where is he?'

Cunningham laughed quietly to himself, but then he stopped laughing. Someone called out hear the bottom of the wall: 'There he is! On the wall! Shoot him.

He heard the sound of a shot, but nothing hit him.

'The war has now come to Colport,' he thought, pulling out his gun. He could not see anyone at first. But then something moved under a tree. At the same time he heard another shot, and something hit the back of his coat.

'That was a near thing!' he thought. He had to get away at once.

It was some time before he moved again, but then he found his piece of wood and got back to the top of the tree. He left the wood up there, got down to the ground, and ran off to his car. He could hear angry cries from *Mandalay*, but he jumped into the car and went off as fast as he could. He was far away on the country roads before the men could start one of their own cars.

He turned his car to the left along a small road, and then to the right along another. He took a lot of small roads until he was far away from Colport. Then he stopped to look back, but he could not see any cars. He was happier now, and was glad to get away from those men.

He started again and then saw a car far away on a road to the right. He stopped and waited. He could hear talking and he saw a policeman speaking to some people in the car.

The police were looking for him! But they did not know his face. No one saw it at *Mandalay*, and he was glad of that.

He turned to the left and was soon a long way from the policeman. Some time later he came to a big road that he knew. He turned along it and went back to Colport.

Near his house he saw a policeman walking quietly along the street. So he turned the car along a smaller road, went to a hotel called "The White Dog" and sat down in it to have a drink. He read a newspaper that he found on a table, and he spoke to two or three people there. Then he walked out quietly.

Two policemen were getting out of a car in front of the hotel, so he turned back and hid under some trees. They went into the hotel, and he walked to his car.

He went to another hotel, "The Two Brothers," but soon the police came in and asked the people there a lot of questions. One of them talked to Cunningham.

'How long have you been here, sir?' he asked.

'Not long,' Cunningham said. 'I've just come in. I want a drink. Why do you want to know?'

'Where were you before you came here?' the policeman asked.

'In another hotel. Why?'

'Which hotel, sir?'

' "The White Dog." '

'Will you come with me, sir? We'll just go back there and ask some questions.'

'But I want a drink. I told you.'

'Yes, sir. But I must ask you to come with me.'

'What's the matter?' said Cunningham.

The policeman did not answer, and soon they were in the other hotel. The policeman asked some of the people there to look at Cunningham's face.

'Have you seen this man before, sir?' the policeman asked one of the people, a man with a very red face.

'Who? Me? No. I've never seen him in my life.'
The man took a long drink and began to talk to someone else.

The policeman put the same question to a lot of
others, and at last one man said, 'Oh, yes. I've seen
him before. He was reading a newspaper in here. On
that chair there, near the table.'

Another man said the same, and the policeman could
not make them change their answers. He was not
pleased, but he had to let Cunningham go. As he went
out of the hotel, he looked back at Cunningham from
the door.

Cunningham did not go home at once. He did not
want the police to see him. He had to take the paper to
Miller, and he did not want the police to be there when
he did it. So he waited.

An hour later he went home in the car and had something to eat. Then he walked to Miller's house and
gave Miller the paper.

'Here it is, Miller,' he said. 'I nearly paid for it with
my life.'

'Only one?' said Miller, taking it. He was angry.

'Yes. Only one. I had no time to look for the others.
But one's better than none at all.'

'You're very late,' Miller said. 'Where have you
been? Look at the time!'

Cunningham sat down. 'Thanks,' he said.

'Thanks for what?'

'For asking me to sit down,' said Cunningham.
'You're most kind. I'm very tired.'

'I didn't ask you to sit down,' said Miller.

'No, you didn't. And why not? Do you always let
your friends stand up when they come to see you?'

'You're not a friend,' said Miller. His face was
angry.

'No, I'm not. How glad I am! You'll never see me again after this. I was nearly caught in that place. Those men came after me with guns. They tried to kill me, but I got the paper for you. Next time you can go yourself. I'm not going there again. Never again!'

'But why are you so late?' Miller asked, as he began to open the paper.

'I told you. Those men were coming after me. Did you want me to bring them here, my dear Miller? To your house? I had to lose them. So I went a long way into the country. They had some cars at *Mandalay*, but I was very quick, and they couldn't find me. After I lost them, I came quietly back to Colport and showed myself in two hotels. I had to buy some drinks – and I'll want some money from you for those. Remember to pay me. Then the police asked everyone a lot of questions.'

'The police!'

'Oh, you're beginning to understand the troubles of my life, are you? You have a good life yourself, don't you, Miller? You just sit quietly in your own house and wait for other men to bring things to you. No police come here, do they? Very nice! You do nothing yourself. Have you ever heard the sound of a shot?'

The paper in Miller's hands was now open and he looked down at it. Then, with a cry, he jumped to his feet.

'What's this?' he cried angrily. 'What have you brought? I don't want this. Have you read it?'

'Oh, I always sit down on the road and read papers when I'm running away from men with guns. What do you think? I have *not* read it. What do I care about it? You've got it now and my part in the work's finished.'

'But it isn't the right paper,' Miller cried angrily.

'Oh yes, it's the right paper. It's some notes about

15

a war meeting. It says so at the top. And it's about ships. I saw the words with my own eyes. What more do you want?'

'But these are the notes for the newspapers!' Miller cried. He was standing up now, and he was a very angry man. 'We don't want these. They're not the full notes which were taken at the meeting. Look at them!'

He put the open paper in front of Cunningham's eyes.

'What?' cried Cunningham. He took the paper and looked down at it. For the first time he began to read it:

WAR MEETING SQP 507 (SHIPS)

Question: What is the next thing?
Answer: —
Question: How many — shall we get before —?
Answer: More than —
Question: Which ships are leaving from —?
Answer: —, —, —, and a lot of others.
Question: And how many from —?
Answer: — or —.
Question: Which ship's taking the — to —?
Answer: The —.
Question: When will it leave?
Answer: On —.
Question: At what time?
Answer: —.

Fathers and Sons

'COME in, Harry,' said Peter Everton kindly at the front door.

He took his old friend into the sitting-room, and they sat down in front of the fire. Their wives were in London, and the two men liked a talk when they had the time. Their sons were running about outside the windows.

Everton sat down, but he looked through the window first.

'My son George has nothing in his head,' he said sadly. 'George can't think at all. Every other boy in the town has a better head than George. Poor boy! What kind of life is he going to have? I wanted him to be a doctor, but he'll never be a doctor. Doctors have to think.' He laughed sadly.

'Oh, he can't be as bad as my boy Vernon,' said Harry Glossop. 'Vernon has never been a thinker and he never will be one. It's very sad. He'll never be rich. He'll be poor all his life.'

'Your Vernon must be a lot better than my George,' said Everton. He did not know much about Vernon, but he knew his own son well. 'No one can be as bad as George. His head's made of wood. Let me show you.'

He opened the window and asked George to come in.

The boy soon ran into the room. His face was red and he looked happy.

'George,' said his father, 'what did you say yesterday about a car? Do you want a new car?'

'Oh, yes please, Father. A big car, please. A car for myself.'

'But you're too young to own a car.'

'Oh, that doesn't matter,' said George.

'But the laws of England don't let small boys own cars.'

'Oh, I don't care about the laws,' said George. 'So can I have a big car, please? A red one?'

Everton took out a pound note and gave it to his son. 'Here's a pound,' he said. 'I was in the town this morning, and I saw some big new cars in a flower shop in Hudson Street. Do you know Hudson Street?'

'Oh yes, Father.'

'Right! Take this pound note and go to the flower shop. You'll see a lot of cars there. Buy the car that you like best.'

The boy thanked his father, took the pound note and ran happily out of the room. The two men could see him through the window. They boy ran into the road and turned along it with the pound note in his hand.

'You see?' said Everton, looking at his friend. 'George wants to buy a car for a pound, and he's going to a flower shop to buy it. What has he got in his head?'

'Oh,' said Harry. 'My Vernon's just the same. I'll show you.'

He called his son into the room.

'Vernon, my boy,' said Harry Glossop kindly, 'do you remember Rope Street?'

'In the town, Father? Oh yes. You work there, don't you?'

'That's right. I want you to go there at once. Your mother wants me to go home. She has just telephoned. Our house is on fire. It isn't very late yet and I may still be at work in Rope Street. So go and look there.

The two boys were walking along the road

19

If I'm still there, please tell me to go home at once. Be as quick as you can!'

The boy went out and ran along the road after his friend George. Glossop looked at Everton sadly.

'What do you think of that?' he asked.

'Yes,' said Everton. 'That was bad, wasn't it? He didn't think very quickly then, did he?'

'He didn't think at all. He never thinks. He can't think. He'll run all the way to Rope Street, but he'll not find me there. So he'll run all the way back here to tell me the great news.'

The two boys were walking along the road and talking.

'My father can't think very well,' said George. 'He gave me a pound to buy a car at a flower shop. But it's a long way to the flower shop, and he gave me nothing to pay for a taxi. I must keep the pound to pay for the car, so I'll have to walk all the way there. Then, after I buy the car, I'll have to walk all the way back. Why couldn't he give me some more money?'

'You're right,' said Vernon, walking by his side. 'Men can't think. They don't even try. My father's just as bad as yours. He told me to go to Rope Street to find him. Mother wants him to go home. Our house is on fire. But it'll take me nearly an hour to walk to Rope Street, and there was a telephone on the table near his chair. He knew about it, too, because Mother telephoned to him about the fire. He said so. Why didn't he telephone to Rope Street and tell himself to go home? He could do that very quickly. But now he'll have to wait for an hour or more before I tell him about the house. So the fire will burn the house to the ground. It makes me very angry. Men can't think, can they?'

In the Train

FIONA Ingram sometimes went by train from Sitting-ford to see her sister, Celia. Celia lived at Hurton, a town a long way from Sittingford. Sometimes Celia came to Fiona's house, but she was a married woman and had a lot of work to do at home.

The sisters liked to meet when they could. They liked to have a talk, and sometimes they met to have dinner at a hotel. Unlike many sisters, they were good friends.

One day Fiona caught her train at Sittingford station and sat down in it, putting her handbag by her side. One other woman got in after Fiona and sat down without speaking. She had a handbag, too. Most women have. There was no one else there when the train started.

The noise of the train on the line made Fiona sleepy and she shut her eyes. She was soon asleep, but she did not sleep very long.

Her handbag was open when she opened her eyes again, and she thought at once about her money.

She always carried a five-pound bank-note when she made journeys away from Sittingford, and she always put one in her bag when she went to see Celia.

She looked inside the bag. She could not see the five-pound note. She looked again, moving things about quickly in the bag. There were some small things that girls always carry about and there were some one-pound notes. But there was no five-pound note.

'Someone has taken it out of my bag!' she thought angrily, looking at the other woman's face. The woman was asleep. She had a sad white face and a cut over one eye, and she was not at all beautiful.

Fiona waited quietly, but the woman did not move so Fiona stood up, quietly opened the woman's handbag and looked inside. Yes! On the top of the other things there was a five-pound note! Quickly and quietly she took it out and put it into her own bag. Then she moved back to her place and sat down again.

'You are not the only woman,' she thought, 'who can take money out of handbags in trains!'

She shut her eyes and kept them shut. But she was not asleep.

The woman stood up when the train stopped at the next station. It was Longton Green, a small town with some shops in it. The woman got out. She did not open her bag or speak to Fiona.

'She'll open it and look inside when she gets to a shop or when she gets home,' Fiona thought. 'She's not as rich as she thinks!'

Fiona's station, Hurton, was the next, and she left the train and walked to Celia's house. The two girls sat down by the fire to talk, and Fiona told her sister about the woman in the train.

'Never sleep in a train, Celia,' she said. 'You have to keep your eyes open. Thieves go by train like everyone else.'

Later in the day Fiona went back home. She opened the door of her small sitting-room.

What did she think when she saw her five-pound note on the table? It was partly hidden under a book.

Her heart jumped, and she stood and looked down at the note. Then she remembered. 'I put it there ready to take this morning,' she thought. 'But I left it there and went without it. So that woman wasn't a thief at all!'

She sat down. 'I'm a thief myself,' she thought sadly. 'I took that woman's money. Oh, what shall I do?'

She opened her bag and looked inside. Yes! There was the woman's note. Where could she put it? What could she do with it? She must find the woman and give the note back to her. But how could she find her?

She took the woman's five-pound note into her bedroom. There was a small lamp on the table near the bed and there was a red cloth on the table under the lamp. She took the lamp off the table, hid the woman's money under the cloth and put the lamp back.

Then she went back to the sitting-room and sat down by the fire to think.

How was she going to find the woman? She did not know her name. And where did she live? In Sittingford? In Longton Green? The woman got out of the train at Longton Green, but was she going home or was she just going there to the shops or to meet a friend? It was hard to answer these questions.

Fiona sat looking into the fire for some time. Then she went back to the station, took a train to Longton Green and walked about the streets there for some hours. She looked at women's faces in all kinds of places, but she did not see that sad white face again. So she took the last train back to Sittingford and went quietly to bed.

'That journey didn't help much!' she thought as she shut her eyes.

On the next day she walked about Sittingford until her feet were tired. She did not see the woman with the white face.

After this she often went by train to Longton Green. She always left the woman's money under the lamp in the bedroom because she did not want to lose it. She could bring the woman back to the house when she found her.

She did not find her.

She went to other towns near Longton Green. She looked in stations and along country roads. She looked at women's faces in trains, in banks, in fish shops, in dress shops, in bookshops. She looked in the windows of cars that went along the roads. She never saw the woman with the white face. She got very tired, and she was getting poorer and poorer. When she went to other towns, every train journey cost money.

She thought of the police. If a woman loses some money, she may tell the police. But Fiona did not want to meet the police. She was very like a thief.

One day she saw a woman's back outside a bread shop and she ran along the road and looked at the woman's face. But it was not the right face. It was another woman and she did not look pleased when she saw Fiona's eyes looking into her own.

That night Fiona sat down to think. 'If I never find her,' she thought, 'it'll save me a lot of trouble. I can keep the five pounds. I can buy a lot of things with five pounds and I am poorer now than I was.'

But she could not keep the money, and she knew it.

She wrote a letter to the *Sittingford News*, the town's newspaper. She told the story, but did not like to put her own name at the end of the letter. So she wrote 'An unhappy girl' in the place of the name.

'If the woman from the train reads this,' she wrote in the letter, 'let her stand outside the Overseas Bank in Sittingford at any time in the afternoon of any day. The writer of this letter will see her there and will bring her the five pounds.'

Fiona could see the bank from her front window, but she never saw her letter in the *Sittingford News*. The

It was not the right face

writer's name was not given, so the newspaper did not put it in.

At last she could not try any more. One morning she took the five-pound note from under the cloth by the bed and took it to the police station. She showed it to a young policeman there and told him the story from beginning to end.

'Please sit down,' he said. 'I'll tell Mr Fetter about this.'

He walked to a door, opened it and went into the room. Fiona sat down to wait. She could hear the two men talking quietly in the room. Then the policeman came back and asked her to go in.

'Mr Fetter will see you now,' he said.

Fetter asked her to sit down and tell the story again. When she came to the end of it, he said, 'Why didn't you come to us before?'

'I didn't want anyone to know anything about it,' she said sadly. 'I took some money when I didn't own it. I'm a thief! I didn't want to tell you or anyone else.'

'Yes,' he said, 'I can understand that. You make it very hard for me. You've stolen some money, haven't you? Please show me the note. Have you brought it with you?'

She opened her bag and gave it to him. 'Will you have to keep me here?' she asked sadly.

Fetter was looking at the note with some care. He put it in the strong light from the window and then he looked at the back of it. Then he put it down on the table and turned to Fiona.

'No,' he said. 'We shall not have to keep you here today. You can go home, but you must come back to-morrow. Where do you live?'

She told him and he wrote it down.

'No one has come here to tell us about this lost note,' he said, looking at her quietly.

'But when some money's stolen, don't the losers come to tell the police?'

'Yes, they do,' he said. 'But this woman hasn't come here. We knew nothing about this before. Why didn't she come to tell us? That's a question that must be answered, mustn't it? Can you think of an answer?'

'This isn't the only police station in the country,' Fiona said. 'There are hundreds of them. So the woman went to another.'

'All police stations have telephones,' he said, looking at the telephone on his own table. 'When any money's stolen, every police station is told about it. We've heard nothing here.'

He asked her to leave the note with him and to come back in the morning. 'I just want to telephone to some other police stations,' he said, 'and to talk to a banker about this.'

'A banker?' she cried.

But he said no more.

On the next day she went to the police station again and Fetter took her into his room.

'I have some news for you,' he said. 'Please sit down.'

'Have you found the owner?' she cried. 'You've been very quick.'

'No, no. We haven't found her.' The five-pound note was on the table and he took it and turned it over in his hands.

'This is the note that you brought to me yesterday,' he said. 'It's bad. It didn't come from the Bank of England or from any other bank. It isn't a bank-note. It looks like one, but no one who understands bank-notes will give you anything for it. It isn't money at all. It's only paper.'

At first she did not move or speak. Then she said, 'Oh! Only paper? I never thought of that! I took great care of it and hid it under a lamp.' She gave a little laugh.

'That woman never came here to tell us about the stolen note,' Fetter said, 'and now we understand that very well, don't we? It's a bad note and she knew it. She didn't want the police to know about her or to find her. This must be true if your story's true.'

He stopped to look at her face. 'You don't make bad money yourself, do you?' he said.

She was very angry. 'Please come and look in my house at once,' she said.

'I don't want to do that,' he said. 'People who make bad money don't often take it to the police and show it to them. I believe your story. So now we have to think hard. That woman may have a lot more bad notes. We must find her.'

'But where is she?' Fiona asked. 'I can't find her. I've tried for a long time in a lot of places. I don't even know her name.'

'She may not live in this part of the country at all,' he said. 'She may be the wife of a man who makes bad notes. She may buy things with them in other parts of the country. She may go anywhere.'

'If she doesn't live here,' said Fiona, 'you'll never find her.'

'It'll be hard to find her,' he said, 'but we'll do our best. Leave the note with me. You can't buy anything with it. If I hear any news, I'll telephone to you. And there's another thing. You're not a thief. You didn't steal any money, did you? Only a piece of paper with some words on it.'

She laughed. 'I'm glad about that,' she said. 'Thank you, Mr Fetter. You've been very kind about all this.'

She went home and stopped thinking about that white face so often. Fetter never telephoned to her.

A year later she was reading a newspaper one morning and she saw some news from Scotland. A car on the road from Glasgow to Aberdeen hit a tree and was later found in a field near the road.

The man inside was still alive, but he could not move. His face and hands were badly cut and a doctor was called. The police were soon there too and, with a lot of care and trouble, the man was pulled out of the car. He told the doctor his name.

'Lawrence Polgate,' he said. 'I live at 104 Brant Street, Aberdeen.'

After he was carried away, the police had a good look at the car. They found Polgate's clothes in a bag, two books and some food for the journey. In the back of the car they found two other bags and these were full of bad bank-notes.

They took them to the man's house in Aberdeen. The door was opened by a woman with a sad white face.

'Mrs Polgate?' said one of the policemen.

'That's right,' she answered. 'What's the matter?'

'Do you know anything about these bags?' he asked. 'They were found in Mr Polgate's car.'

A very troubled look came into her eyes. 'Where is he?' she cried. 'Is he dead?'

'He isn't dead, Mrs Polgate. But please answer my question. Do you know anything about these bags and the notes in them?'

She did not want to answer, and they took her to the police station. Then they went back to the house in Brant Street and found hundreds of bad notes in a back room of the house.

After Fiona saw this news in the paper, she went to talk to Fetter.

'I'm not very glad about it,' she said. 'I'm sorry for that woman. She looked so sad in the train and she's still sad.'

'She'll soon be a lot sadder,' said Fetter with a hard look in his eyes. 'She's the wife of a thief and she carried bad money about the country. Her troubles, and those of Mr Polgate, are just beginning.'

How did He Do It?

ONE morning Tom Fetter came out of his room at Sittingford Police Station just as a big man was coming in at the front door. As soon as Fetter saw his face, he stopped.

'Charlie Boyd!' he cried. 'What are you doing here? Have you left London?'

Boyd laughed as he took Fetter's hand. They were old friends.

'I haven't left London at all,' he said. 'I'm going back there tomorrow.'

Fetter took his friend into his room and they sat down.

'I want your help, Tom,' Boyd said. 'Is that man Bristow still living in the town?'

'The thief? Yes, he lives here.'

Bristow was a man who was well known to Boyd and the other police. He was a thief and they all knew that, but they could never catch him when he was stealing things. So he just laughed at the police and lived the life of a rich man.

'Have you ever caught him stealing anything?' Boyd asked.

'Never. But he still does it. We know that.'

'Yes. He stole some money last night in London.'

'London?' Fetter cried. 'How do you know that? He was here yesterday. I was talking to him myself about some street lights.'

'The night is long, Tom. It happened like this. Some money was stolen last night from Alloway Parr's house – a lot of money – about seven hundred pounds.'

31

'Who's Parr? I don't know him.'

'He's a rich builder,' said Boyd. 'He had some money in his house to pay some of his men. He often does that. One of my best men has seen Bristow outside Parr's London house two or three times lately.'

'What was he doing?' Fetter asked.

'Reading a newspaper on the other side of the street. Why does a man go to London just to read a newspaper? My man stopped near the place and waited. He saw Bristow looking at the windows of Parr's house. He read the newspaper a little and then looked over the top at the house.'

'A man may look at a house if he likes,' said Fetter.

'Yes, Tom. But this morning the money wasn't there. The work looks like Bristow's work. The window was opened just as Bristow opens windows. It was a bedroom window and Bristow likes bedroom windows. He can get up the side of a house better than anyone else. So we're all thinking of Bristow. The man who stole this money went up to the window, cut the glass, opened the window and got into the bedroom. Then he went down to the sitting-room to look for the money. He often works like this. He found the money. It was hidden under a lot of letters on a table, and Bristow took it all. There are other things that make us think of Bristow, too.'

'But he lives here now – in Hill Road.'

'Is he here today?' Boyd asked.

'I haven't seen him today, but he was here yesterday, as I told you. We can go to his house now if you like.'

'If he's there,' said Boyd, 'he has come back. He went to London last night and came back after he stole the money. I've looked at the times of the trains from here to London and back. There's one in the afternoon to London, but there are no trains late at night to bring him back. So he went by road.'

'Oh,' said Fetter, 'he never goes by train. He always goes in that great car of his. At what time was the money taken?'

'Parr hid it before he went to bed. He was going to pay his men this morning. But when he went to get it, it wasn't there. The window glass was cut, too. So the money was stolen in the night, but we don't know the time. No one saw anything from outside.'

'Bristow came to the police station yesterday just after the sun went down,' said Fetter. 'Two of the street lamps near his house were giving no light. I went with him to look at them. So he wasn't in London then. But let us go to his house and talk to him. He'll not want to tell us anything, but we may see something that will help.'

It was raining when they went outside to Boyd's car. A policeman, Atkins, was waiting in it. The car took them to a pretty little road and stopped outside a house there.

'This is Bristow's house,' Fetter said as they got out, 'and that's his car.'

A big blue car was standing at the right-hand side of the house.

'It isn't very beautiful,' said Fetter, 'but it's very fast. He always keeps it at the side of the house like that.'

Bristow was at home, but he did not try to help them much.

'I wasn't in London yesterday,' he said. 'I was here. Mr Fetter saw me. What's the matter?'

They did not answer his question.

'Have you a lot of money in the house just now?' said Boyd.

Bristow did not try to help them much

'Not much. No. You can look if you like, but you'll find very little.'

They went into two or three of the rooms, but then Bristow asked them to leave. 'I have a lot to do today,' he said.

He opened the front door for them and they went outside. It was still raining. They looked again at the big car. It was wet, but not very dirty.

'You didn't take the car to London yesterday at all?' said Boyd.

'No.'

'So it was here all day? Morning? Afternoon? Night?'

'All day and all night,' said Bristow, 'and I'm getting wet.' He turned, went back into the house and shut the front door.

The two friends went back to Atkins and the police car.

'That hasn't helped us much,' said Fetter.

'I have to go to Portsmouth today,' said Boyd. 'Will you ask some questions in the town about Bristow? I didn't like his way of speaking. He was trying to hide something. I could see that from his eyes, too. What was he hiding?'

'I don't know,' said Fetter.

'On my way back to London tomorrow,' said Boyd, 'I'll stop at the police station to see you. You may have some news.'

After Boyd left for Portsmouth, Fetter went to his room and called Harding and Walton, two of his best men. He told them to find out everything about Bristow.

'You, Harding, go into the town and ask questions about Bristow and that great blue car of his. It's a car that people can see, isn't it? I want to know all about it. Did anyone see it yesterday? At what time? Where? Did anyone see it last night? Was it standing near his house all night? Anything like that.'

He turned to the other policeman as Harding went out.

'And you, Walton, wait near Bristow's house, but don't let him see you. If he goes out for a walk, go after him. Keep a fast police car near you. If he goes out in that car of his, go after him. You mustn't lose him. I want to know everything that he does.'

The man went off, and Fetter looked at the times of the trains to and from London. There was a good train to London in the afternoon, but no trains came to Sittingford late at night.

Later in the day Harding came back with some news for Fetter.

'Bristow's car never left the house yesterday, sir,' he said. 'Four people saw it near his house – one in the morning, one in the afternoon and two late at night.'

'What kind of people are they? Do you believe them?'

'Yes, I believe them all, sir. Mrs Freeth was one, and we can believe her. A girl going home from work saw it there, too. Young Lister saw the car there very late last night when he was walking home from a friend's house. We can believe him, too. It's true, sir. The car was here all the time.'

'It takes two hours to go from here to London,' said Fetter, 'and two hours to come back.'

'And an hour to steal the money, sir,' said Harding.

'Yes. That's five hours. I saw the man myself when he was angry about the street lamps.'

'And Lister saw the car there about four hours later,' said Harding. 'So the car didn't take him to London.'

'The car's clean, too,' said Fetter. 'So it didn't go along a lot of dirty roads last night. Or did he clean it after he came home? Did he go all the way to London after Lister saw the car? Did he steal the money and come back here and then clean the car? Clean it well? So well that we didn't see any dirt on it today? Did anyone see him cleaning it?'

'I haven't found anyone who saw him cleaning it, sir. When these people saw the car, it was just standing there near the house. They all say the same thing.'

'He didn't go to London by train,' said Fetter. 'I've had a look at the times of the trains. Bristow came here to talk about those street lamps, and the last train to London leaves Sittingford before then. So he wasn't on it. So he didn't go by train and he didn't go by road.

He didn't walk to London and back, did he? It's too far.'

'He could go to the London road and stand there and wait, sir. Then he could stop a car on its way to London and go in it. A lot of people do that.'

'At night?' said Fetter. 'And then did Bristow stop another kind person on the Sittingford road and ask him to bring him back here? When he was carrying seven hundred pounds? Stolen money? No, no. I can't believe it.'

'You're right, sir. Thieves don't work like that, but I can't think of any other way. He's not a bird. Did he go in a stolen car?'

'There have been no stolen cars for a long time. And he didn't stand on the road to stop a car. Any man who's stopped like that will remember it. And Bristow never works with others. He always works alone. You'll not find anyone who took him to London by road last night. I know that man well.'

Harding went out, and Fetter thought quietly about Bristow. No one could ever catch that man. It was always the same. He stole things and the police knew it. But he was never seen and he was never caught.

'Bristow didn't go to London,' Fetter thought a long time later. 'Someone else stole the seven hundred pounds. Charlie Boyd's not right this time.'

Charlie Boyd himself came to the police station on the next day and asked Fetter for news.

'No news,' said Fetter sadly. 'Bristow's car was here all day and all night. So he didn't go in it. And he didn't go by train. The last train left when Bristow was still here – in the police station. He was talking about those lamps. So another man in London stole that money, Charlie. It wasn't Bristow this time.'

Just then they heard a noise outside the room and

Fetter opened the door to look out. He saw Bristow there, talking angrily. Walton was there too, with some other men of the police station. Bristow was making a lot of noise.

'What's the matter, Walton?' Fetter called. 'Come in here.'

Walton came in. There was a cut on the side of his face.

'Sit down there,' said Fetter, 'and tell us.'

'I was standing outside Bristow's house, sir, as you told me. He came out and walked down the road to the river. I went after him, but he didn't see me. I walked quietly and hid when I could. He went to that broken old building down by the river. It has a big old wooden door, as you remember, sir. Bristow opened the door and went inside.'

'What did you do then?' Fetter asked. Boyd said nothing.

'I went quietly to the door, sir, and looked inside. There wasn't much light and at first I could only see some dirty pieces of cloth. Then I saw something under the cloth. It was a car, sir – as I was able to see later. It was well hidden under that cloth, so no one could see it at first.'

'Another car!' cried Boyd.

'Yes, sir. Then Bristow turned his head and saw me. He was looking inside the car at the time. He was trying to find something. When he saw me, he was angry and started to fight. But I'm a strong man and so I brought him here.'

'So he has another car!' said Fetter. 'Yes! I'm beginning to understand. We didn't know this. You've done well, Walton. We must go and look at it, mustn't we?'

Fetter stood up, and Boyd stood up with him. They

went out of the police station, leaving Bristow with the other men there.

They got into Boyd's police car and Walton went with them to show them the place. They soon came to the old building and Walton took them to the door. It was still open. They could see a small fast car inside. On the ground near it, there was some dirty cloth.

'It was hidden under that,' said Walton.

'Bring the car outside, Walton,' Boyd said.

Walton started it without trouble, and it was soon on the road near the police car.

'I'll bring it to the police station,' said Fetter. 'Walton, take Mr Boyd back there with you in the other car.'

'Right, sir!'

He took Boyd off to the police station, and Fetter was left alone. There were no other cars in this place and it was very quiet. He got into the small car.

Just when he was starting it, something moved under the trees. The car door was pulled open and Fetter saw Bristow outside.

'Bristow!' cried Fetter. 'How did you get here?'

Bristow had a gun in his hand and it was touching Fetter's arm.

'Get out!' said Bristow.

Fetter was a quick thinker. The door of the car was still open. Before Bristow could do anything, Fetter moved his feet and the car ran quickly back along the road. The door hit Bristow's arm and side and he fell to the ground with a cry.

Fetter stopped the car, jumped out and sat on Bristow before he could stand up again. The gun was far away on the road. At the same time a police car stopped near the two men. There were three other policemen in it and Harding jumped out.

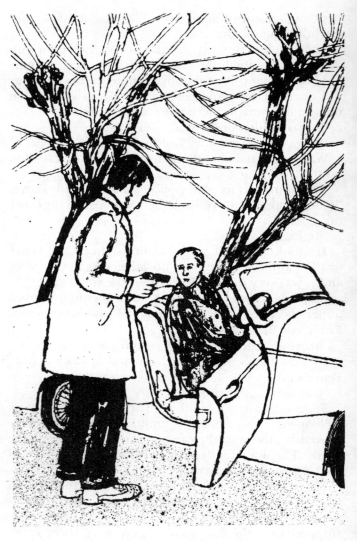

'Get out!' said Bristow

'Bristow got away, sir!' Harding cried. Then he saw the face of the man on the ground. 'Oh, there he is!'

Some time later, two cars stopped outside Sittingford police station and Fetter with the others went in. Bristow was taken into Fetter's room and questioned, but he did not give any answers and so he was taken away.

'We didn't see him stealing the money,' said Fetter, after Bristow was taken out. 'He fought a policeman, and we can keep him here for that, but where's the money? Where's the seven hundred pounds?'

'It must be in that small car,' said Boyd. 'Bristow was looking for something in it. Walton saw him.'

He turned to Walton. 'Go and look,' he said.

Walton went out. Some time later he came back. He had seven hundred pounds in his hands.

Dead or Alive?

DEREK Melville looked sadly through the window at the rain. He was not very pleased this morning. He was a writer, but his book was not going well. How could he write well when that talker, Trevor White, was staying in the house? The man talked and talked. There was no end to his talking and not a word of it could help anyone.

Two years before this Melville came to stay in the house of his old friend Henry White. White asked him to come because the house was too big for himself alone and his wife was now dead. So Melville was given a small bedroom and he had a table for his work at one side of the sitting-room.

There he did a lot of good work in the happier days, but when Trevor White came to stay with his brother Henry, the happier days were at an end.

Trevor once lived in Italy, but he left that country because it did not like him. So he went to live in Spain, but Spain was another country that did not like him. So he left Spain, too. He tried a lot of other countries, but he always had to leave. Now he was staying with his brother in Tambridge, not because he liked Tambridge, but because he had no home of his own.

He was never pleased and he had no work to do. So he was nearly always in the house and nearly always talking. He did not like Tambridge or the shops in it. He did not like the people of the town or their children. He did not like the rain. He wanted to live under a hot sun, but the sun here, when he saw it, was cold. The nights were often cold, too. He did not like English food.   There was only one bank and it was too small for him. He liked big banks. He did not like the trees that grew in Tambridge.   He did not like anything and he did not stop saying so.

Derek Melville was tired of Trevor the Talker, but at first he said nothing. He kept quiet about it because the house was not his. But he was unable to write good books now; sometimes he could not write anything at all, good or bad. As soon as he began to write, Trevor came into the sitting-room and talked about nothing for hours.

Melville turned away from the window, went up to his bedroom and sat down. He had to think. He had to make a change of some kind.

After dinner he had a talk with his friend Henry. 'I must look for a house of my own,' he said. 'I never write much here now and a change will be a good thing.'

Henry was sorry. He wanted his old friend to stay, but he was a man who understood things. So Melville took a train to another part of England, a long way from Tambridge and from Trevor the Talker. He got out of the train at Hamdon, went to a hotel and started to look at small houses in the town and near it.

He could not find the kind of house that he wanted, so he moved to another town. He moved again soon after that and then again; and so at last he came to Rockergate, not far from Winchester.

He stayed the night in one of the hotels and in the morning he walked through the streets, looking at houses. He found one in Green Street that he liked and stopped to look at it. He could see some tables and chairs through the front window, but he saw no one inside.

The name of the house was *Blue Flowers*. He did not

The name of the house was Blue Flowers

like the name, but a name changes nothing. It was a quiet street. A writer likes quiet places.

As he stood there thinking, a man with a red face stopped by his side.

'Nice house!' said the man.

'Very nice,' Melville answered.

'Are you looking for a house?' the man asked.

'Yes, if it's quiet. I'm a writer.'

'The man who lived in this house was a writer, too. His name was Lionel Bruce. Have you read any of his books? They're good.'

'No, I don't think so. I don't remember the name.'

'He'll never want the house again,' the man said.

'Why?' said Melville. 'Is he dead?'

'They say so. He went off to New Zealand last year. He wanted to write a book about people who live in

Auckland, but he never came back. We've heard no news of him – no letters – nothing. You'll be able to buy the house if you want it. I know something about it. My name's Tenterden.'

'Thank you, Mr Tenterden. My name's Melville. Who owns the house now? Was it Bruce's own house?'

'No. It's his wife's. They lived in it before he went off. She didn't want to go to New Zealand. It's a long way, Mr Melville. She has another house too. She lives in it now – in Ollendale, not far from here. She wants to sell this house. She hasn't got a lot of money.'

'Do you know her?' Melville asked.

'Oh, yes. I know her well. I live here, but I often go to Ollendale. I'm going there this afternoon. You can come with me in the car if you like. I'll take you to her house there and you can talk to her about *Blue Flowers*.'

And so, later in the day, Melville met Mrs Bruce in her house at Ollendale. It was a small house and she did not look rich, but it was not old. She wanted to sell *Blue Flowers* as soon as she could and she wanted to sell everything in it at the same time.

'That will help me, Mr Melville,' she said. 'I'm an old woman and I don't like trouble. You can go into the house and look at it at any time. It's not a bad house, but it's older than this one. Lionel liked it very much, but I never liked it myself. I like new houses better. Look at this floor. It's good, isn't it? And beautiful. The wood isn't falling to pieces. But Lionel had to pay a builder to do a lot of work in that other house. But that didn't matter to him. He was always ready to pay people. He didn't care about money and he didn't like saving.' She spoke sadly.

'He was a writer, wasn't he?'

'Yes. He got a lot of money for his books, but he

liked buying things at the shops, and he never had much in the bank.'

'Did he write a lot of books?'

'Yes, a lot. But there was one which never got to the bookshops.'

'Oh! Why was that?'

'I don't know. I never understood it. He wrote a book called *Five Journeys*. I know that because he sometimes talked to me about it and I often saw him at work on it. But no one has ever seen the book itself, or read it.'

'Never? Where is it?'

'I don't know. He wrote it and finished it and then he lost all the papers. Every one! He looked for them but he never found them.'

'Did he often lose things?' Melville asked. He did not care very much about all this, but the old woman wanted to talk. People who live alone like talking.

'Yes,' she answered. 'He often lost things. He didn't take much care of his things. He was very sorry about *Five Journeys*. But he never found the papers and then he went away to New Zealand. It was a sad thing. He was going to look for them when he came home, but he never came home.'

'I'm very sorry,' said Melville.

'Oh, I'm taking all your time,' she said. 'You don't want to hear this old story. But now I'm alone and I'll never want the things in that other house. If you buy it, you can buy the things in it too. I'll be glad to sell them.'

'And I'll be glad to buy them,' he said, 'if I buy the house.'

'Good. Please go into it when you like. Mr Tenterden will do anything that you want. He does a lot of things for me and you can ask him any questions about it.'

He thanked the old woman and left. Tenterden took

46

him back to Rockergate, opened the house for him and then went home.

Melville had a good look inside the house. He liked it, but the rooms were dirty.

'No one has lived here for some time,' he thought.

There was a room at the back of the house which he liked very much. It was just the right place for him. There were some old books and newspapers on the floor near the door, but he could take those away. There was an old and beautiful writing-table in the room and there was a big chair near the window. He was pleased when he saw the chair.

'Just the place for an afternoon's sleep!' he thought with a quiet laugh.

From the window he could see trees and flowers. The room was hot because the sun came through the window glass. It was very quiet. When he remembered Trevor the Talker, he laughed.

He had another look at the house on the next day and then went to talk to Tenterden.

'I'll buy the house, Mr Tenterden, he said. 'I like it very much. I shall want the chairs and tables and beds, too; I have none of my own. I'll send you the money for everything as soon as I've been to the bank. But the rooms are dirty, aren't they?'

'Yes. No one has lived there for a long time.'

'Can you tell me of a good woman who'll clean them?'

'Oh, yes. I'll ask Mrs Venner. Mrs Port cleaned that house in the old days, but she has left Rockergate. Mrs Venner often helps people in their houses. She likes to make a little money. Leave it to me. You live in Tambridge, don't you? Are you on the telephone?'

'Yes,' said Melville. 'I'll go back to Tambridge now and wait until you telephone. Many thanks.'

Melville went back to Henry White's house and sent the money. Then one day Tenterden telephoned. 'Mrs Venner's ready to give the house a good clean,' he said. 'Shall I ask her to do it?'

'Please do that. I'll move into the house before the end of the month. Can she do it before then?'

'I'll ask her,' he said.

And so one day Melville got out of a taxi in Green Street, Rockergate, and carried his bags into the house. The door was open and a big woman was waiting for him.

'I'm Mrs Venner, sir,' she said, 'and you're Mr Melville.'

'That's right,' he said.

'I've cleaned most of the rooms, sir, but I haven't finished everything.'

He looked into the sitting-room and was pleased. It was very clean, and he thanked her.

'I've done them all except the back room, sir,' she said.

'The room with the writing-table in it?'

'That's right, Mr Melville. I haven't done that. I saw you there yesterday through the window when you were standing near the door. I came back in the afternoon, but you were still there and so I did something else.'

She did not look very pleased. She was a woman who liked to finish her work and then go home.

'But I don't understand you,' he said. 'I wasn't here yesterday. I've just come by train from Tambridge. I was there yesterday.'

'Oh, were you, sir?' She did not speak again for some time. Then she said, 'So it was someone else! How did he get in? Oh, I remember. The window of the room was open.'

'But why did he want to get in?' said Melville. 'And who was he? Did you know him? Did you see his face?'

'No, I couldn't see his face. I only saw the back of his head.'

They went into the writing room. 'What was the man doing when you saw him the first time?' Melville asked. He did not like this much.

'He was looking at the floor near the door, sir.'

'Nothing else?'

'No, sir. Just standing there and looking down.'

'And what was he doing when you came back in the afternoon?'

'He was still standing near the door. He was looking down at those dirty books there.'

'Still in the same place?'

'Yes, but it doesn't matter, sir. I can give the room a good clean tomorrow. Shall I do that? I have to go home now, but I can come back again tomorrow afternoon.'

'Please do that. And many thanks!'

He carried his bags up to the larger of the two bedrooms and had a wash. Then he went out to buy something to eat.

When he came back he went into the sitting-room and looked at it. 'Home!' he thought. 'And quiet!'

He had some food and went to bed. He slept well and started work on his book on the next day. But when he sat at the writing-table, he could not think about his book. He thought about the man who was looking at the floor near the door.

Why did he look there? And who was this man?

Melville had a look at the floor there himself, but he could only see the wood and the old newspapers with

49

the books on them. He sat down in the big chair to think.

From the chair he could see the door of the room. As he sat there thinking, he saw something moving outside the door. He looked again.

A small dog looked into the room, stopped at the door, turned, and then walked quietly away. It did not make a sound.

Melville did not own a dog and the doors of the house were shut. How did the dog get in? He ran out of the room to catch it, but he could see nothing at all. He went to all the rooms in the house, but there was no dog in them.

He went back to the writing room and looked there again. Nothing!

'I'm seeing things that aren't there!' he thought. He sat down in the big chair. He could not understand this at all.

His eyes turned again to the door and again he saw the dog. This time it came into the room, but when it moved, it did not stand on the floor. He could see the animal's head and ears and he could see the top of its back, but he could not see its feet. They were under the wood of the floor.

As he looked, the dog began to move through the wood to the door and it went quietly out. Again there was no sound.

The floor outside was not as high as the floor of the room and Melville could see the dog's feet when it was outside.

He saw all this from his chair near the window. He could not believe his eyes at first and his heart nearly stopped.

Again he jumped out of the chair and ran after the dog. But he found nothing outside the writing room.

Again he saw the dog

When he came back, the window was open. He ran to the window to look out, but he could see nothing except flowers and trees.

He shut the window. The room was very cold. He put his hands over his eyes to think. This was his new home!

He had no friends in Rockergate, so he went to talk to Tenterden and told him about the dog.

'Walking through the floor!' he said.

'The floor of the writing room?' Tenterden asked.

'Yes. It's higher than the floor outside. The dog's feet were under the floor.'

Tenterden looked quietly through the window. 'That's a new floor in the writing room,' he said. 'One day Bruce put his foot through the old floor. It's an old house and the wood wasn't strong. It was falling to pieces. So he asked Hamilton the builder to put a new floor there. Hamilton made the new floor higher than the old one and Bruce wasn't very pleased about it.'

'When did this happen?'

'Oh, I don't know. Some years ago. About a year after the dog died.'

'Bruce's dog?' Melville asked.

'Yes. He had a small dog.'

'And it died before the new floor was put in?'

'That's right.'

'So the dog never saw the higher floor?'

Tenterden did not answer and the two men looked into the fire for some time. Then Melville spoke again.

'Tell me some more about Bruce,' he said.

'I didn't know much about him. I didn't often go to his house and he never came to see me here. His house was always too cold for me. The windows were always open when I went there. I like a hot fire myself.'

52

'He lost some papers, didn't he?' said Melville. 'Mrs Bruce told me about a book. She called it *Five Journeys*.'

'Yes, I heard about it. He lost those papers before he went to New Zealand. He tried to find them, but he didn't try very hard. He never took care of his things. He often lost books and papers. And then he lost *Five Journeys!* All that work done for nothing! He was going to find the papers when he came home. But if he's dead, he'll never come home. We haven't seen them in the house. Mrs Bruce isn't a rich woman and if we can find them she may be richer. They'll bring her some money when they're made into a book. Bruce was a good writer. People who saw his name on a book bought it. He was always able to sell his books. He could write well; I'll say that for him.'

Tenterden stopped and put a piece of wood on the fire. Then he looked at Melville's face.

'Bruce and his dog have come back, haven't they?' he said quietly.

'I don't like the sound of that,' Melville said.

'They've come back. The man's looking for the papers. He wants them to be a book, like his others. The dog's trying to help him.'

Melville did not speak for some time. Then he said, 'If there is a man in the house and if there is a dog, you may be right.'

'You've seen the dog and Mrs Venner has seen the man.'

'Can we always believe our eyes?' Melville said. 'Two people may look at the same thing, but they may not see the same thing. What is "red"? What is "blue"? Do you know? Try to tell someone about it. Try to tell a man who can't see. You can't do it. I don't always believe my eyes. All this may be only in my own head.

There may be no dog. Have you seen anything in that house?'

'Only chairs and tables,' said Tenterden. 'But I don't often go there.'

'I'm not at all happy about this,' said Melville. 'I can't write when a dog's walking through the floor. What shall I do about it? I don't want to sell the house. I like it.'

'Find the papers,' said Tenterden. 'If you can do that, Bruce and his dog will sleep quietly. I don't know much about these things, but if something's unfinished, a man may want to finish it. If his wife's poor, he'll do his best for her.'

'But he's dead.'

'We don't know that, do we?' said Tenterden. 'We know very little. But find the papers. When we see *Five Journeys* in the bookshops, you'll have a quiet life.'

When Melville went home, he found the window of the writing room open. He shut it sadly once more.

Mrs Venner came in the afternoon to finish her cleaning. She went into the writing room and so Melville went out to buy some bread and other things that he wanted. When he came back, she was looking sad.

'I'm sorry, sir,' she said.

'Why? What's the matter?'

She took him into the writing room and showed him some papers on the floor and on the writing-table.

'There were some books and papers near the door,' she said. 'I had to move them to clean the floor there. All these papers fell out of one of the newspapers.'

Melville's eyes fell on one of the papers. 'Oh!' he cried. 'The lost book! *Five Journeys!*' He took it in his hand and saw the beginning of a story. He looked at Mrs Venner. She was standing near the door with a troubled face.

'Don't be sad, Mrs Venner!' he cried. 'Be glad! You've found a lost book!'

'A book, sir?' she said, looking at the papers.

'Yes. These will be a book soon. They were lost, Mrs Venner. Mr Bruce wrote them and now they'll have to go to London. I must take them there. Next year you'll see the book in the bookshops. It's called *Five Journeys.*'

She did not understand very well, and he could see that.

'Mr Bruce was a writer,' he said. 'He wrote all this and then lost the papers. We can understand that now. He put them in a newspaper to keep them clean. Then he couldn't remember. The newspaper was with these others under those books. So the papers were hidden. When he looked under the books, he couldn't see them. But now you've found them, Mrs Venner!'

She went home with a happier face and Melville went to tell Tenterden. They telephoned to Mrs Bruce at Ollendale.

In the next year Melville bought the book and read it himself. Mrs Bruce grew richer because the book was good and a lot of people heard the story about it and bought it.

Melville never saw the dog again and never again found the window of the writing room open.